Celtic Animals
Coloring Book

Mallory Pearce

DOVER PUBLICATIONS, INC.
Mineola, New York

Bibliographical Note

Celtic Animals Coloring Book is a new work, first published by Dover Publications, Inc., in 1997.

DOVER *Pictorial Archive* SERIES

International Standard Book Number: 0-486-29729-2

Manufactured in the United States of America
Dover Publications, Inc., 31 East 2nd Street, Mineola, N.Y. 11501

Publisher's Note

The name "Celtic" makes us think especially of the British Isles, although the Celts once filled most of Europe—a vast array of tribes speaking different tongues and practicing different traditions.

One highly popular tradition of Celtic design fills the pages of this new book for adventurous colorists of all ages: the Irish "Celtic Revival" tradition of about 800 A.D., associated with the famous Book of Kells. Here is a whole spectrum of ornate, stylized birds, fishes and animals of all sorts, ready for the embellishment of color to come to life on the page.

Most of our Celtic animals live in a dizzying web of interweaving lines as tails, legs, necks and beaks grow to impossible lengths, crossing and recrossing in bizarre patterns. Even a mermaid turns up, swirling endless braids, and two entangled men share the same beard!

Designer Mallory Pearce gives us a wonderful collection full of fantasy, humor and delightful decoration. All that's missing is your imaginative finishing touch of crayons, acrylics or watercolors.

1

3

26